Frankenstein

BY
Mary Shelley

EDITED BY
Philip Page & Marilyn Pettit

ILLUSTRATED BY
Philip Page

Hodder & Stoughton

A MEM   GROUP

Orders: please contact Bookpoint Ltd, 130 Milton Park, Abingdon, Oxon OX14 4SB.
Telephone: (44) 01235 827720, Fax: (44) 01235 400454. Lines are open from 9.00–6.00,
Monday to Saturday, with a 24 hour message answering service. You can also order through
our website at www.hodderheadline.co.uk

British Library Cataloguing in Publication Data
A catalogue record for this title is available from The British Library

ISBN 0 340 78262 5

First published 2001
Impression number   10 9 8 7 6 5
Year   2007 2006 2005 2004

Papers used in this book are natural, renewable and recyclable products. They are made
from wood grown in sustainable forests. The logging and manufacturing processes conform
to the environmental regulations of the country or origin.

Cover illustration by Dave Smith
Artwork by Philip Page
Typeset by Fakenham Photosetting Ltd, Fakenham, Norfolk
Printed in Great Britain for Hodder & Stoughton Educational, a division of Hodder
Headline, 338 Euston Road, London NW1 3BH by J W Arrowsmith Ltd, Bristol.

Contents

About the story

Mary Shelley wrote *Frankenstein* in Switzerland during a wet summer. Her friend Lord Byron challenged four of them to write a **ghost story** each. These would entertain them while they were forced to stay indoors.

She wanted to write a story that would scare readers so much that their blood would chill, their hearts would beat fast and they would be frightened to turn around for fear of what was behind them! One night, she thought up this story and terrified even herself!

She planned it as a short story, but her husband persuaded her to write a full length novel. Since then it has been described as not just a **ghost story** but also a **horror story**. Some people say that it was the first **science-fiction story**!

It has been made into films and comic strips. Nearly every one has heard of Frankenstein! As you read it, decide what **genre** or type of story best describes the book.

As you read, make notes on the parts that frighten you the most. Be prepared to share your ideas at the end!

Cast of characters

Victor Frankenstein
The man who created the
monster.

The monster!

Robert Walton
The man to whom Victor told
the story while on board ship.

Henry Clerval
Victor's friend.

**Alphonse
Frankenstein**
Victor's father.

Ernest
Victor's brother.

William
Victor's brother
who is murdered.

Elizabeth
Victor's cousin and
later his wife.

Justine
A friend who is
wrongly executed.

Mr Kerwin
The magistrate.

Robert Walton writes a letter to his sister. He plans to go to Archangel in Russia, hire a ship and travel to the North Pole.

St Petersburgh
Dec. 11th

I arrived here yesterday. As I walk in the streets of St Petersburgh a cold breeze gives me a foretaste of the pole. I may there discover a passage near the pole.

I am about to proceed on a long and difficult voyage. I shall depart from town in a fortnight or three weeks. My intention is to hire a ship. I do not intend to sail until June.

When shall I return? How can I answer this question! If I succeed, many months, perhaps years, will pass before you and I may meet. If I fail, you will see me again soon, or never. Farewell, my dear Margaret.

Your affectionate brother,
R. Walton

Robert Walton writes that he has a ship, but no real friend. He hopes to set sail soon.

Archangel,
March 28th

How slowly the time passes here! I have hired a vessel and am occupied in collecting my sailors. But I have no friend. I shall certainly find no friend on the wide ocean.

My voyage is only delayed until the weather **shall permit**. The winter has been severe, but the spring promises well. Perhaps I may sail sooner than I expected.

Continue to write to me. I love you. Remember me with affection, should you never hear from me again.

July 7th

My dear sister,

I write a few lines to say that I am safe – and well advanced on my voyage. This letter will reach England by a **merchantman** now on its homeward voyage.

I am in good spirits. **No incidents have hitherto befallen us.**

shall permit – lets us sail (fine weather)   **merchantman** – trading ship
No incidents ... befallen us – nothing has happened to us so far

The ship is trapped in the ice and they see a huge man on a sledge. Later, they pick up another man who has a very strange story to tell.

August 5th

My dear sister,

Last Monday we were surrounded by ice. The mist cleared away. We **perceived** a carriage, fixed on a sledge, drawn by dogs. A being, the shape of a man, but of gigantic stature, sat in the sledge. We watched with our telescopes until he was lost among the distant ice. It was impossible to follow his track.

Before night the ice broke and freed our ship.

In the morning, I found the sailors talking to someone.

Before I come on board **inform me whither you are bound.**

I replied that we were on a voyage of discovery towards the northern pole.

perceived saw   **inform me ... bound** – tell me where you're going

I never saw a man in so wretched a condition.

Two days passed before he was able to speak.

Why had he come so far upon the ice in so strange a vehicle?

To seek one who fled me!

Then I fancy we have seen him!

He asked me questions concerning the route the demon, as he called him, had pursued. I have promised that someone should watch for him and **give him instant notice** if any new object should appear.

August 13th

He is now much recovered. He has asked me many questions and I have related my little history to him.

You have hope. I have lost everything and cannot begin life anew. Listen to my tale.

give him instant notice – tell him immediately

4

Frankenstein tells Walton about his family.

My father was respected by all. One of his friends fell into poverty. He lay on a bed of sickness. His daughter Caroline was occupied in attending him. Her father died. My father came like a protecting spirit to the poor girl. Two years later Caroline became his wife.

My father had a sister. She died and he received a letter from her husband requesting my father to take Elizabeth, the child.

Elizabeth became my playfellow and my friend.

Henry Clerval was the son of a friend of my father. He was constantly with us.

Ernest was six years younger than myself. William was an infant

Such was our domestic circle.

Such was our domestic circle. – this was what our house and family was like

Frankenstein goes to University at Ingolstadt. He meets a man who helps him decide upon his future.

My parents **resolved** that I should become a student at the university of Ingolstadt. My departure was fixed. But before that day could arrive, Elizabeth caught scarlet fever. On the third day, my mother sickened and died calmly.

My journey to Ingolstadt was now again determined upon. The day of my departure arrived. I threw myself into the **chaise** that was to **convey** me away. I was now alone.

I paid a visit to some of the professors. I went into the lecturing room, which **M.** Waldman entered shortly after.

I departed pleased with the professor and his lecture and paid him a visit the same evening. He took me into his laboratory.

It decided my future.

resolved – decided   **chaise** – carriage   **convey** – take   **M** – short for Monsieur (mister)

Frankenstein thinks about making a human being. He visits horrible places and collects foul things before he is ready to try out his idea.

I improved rapidly.
When, I often asked myself **did the principle of life proceed?** It was a mystery. To examine life we must first have death. I saw how man **was wasted**, the change from life to death, and death to life. I was surprised that I alone should discover so astonishing a secret.

After days and nights, I became **capable of bestowing animation upon lifeless matter**. I see that you expect to be informed of the secret. That cannot be; listen until the end of my story.

When ... did the principle of life proceed? – How do we make life?
was wasted – was rotting away   **capable ... matter** – able to bring dead things to life

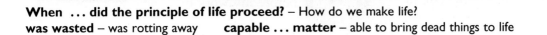

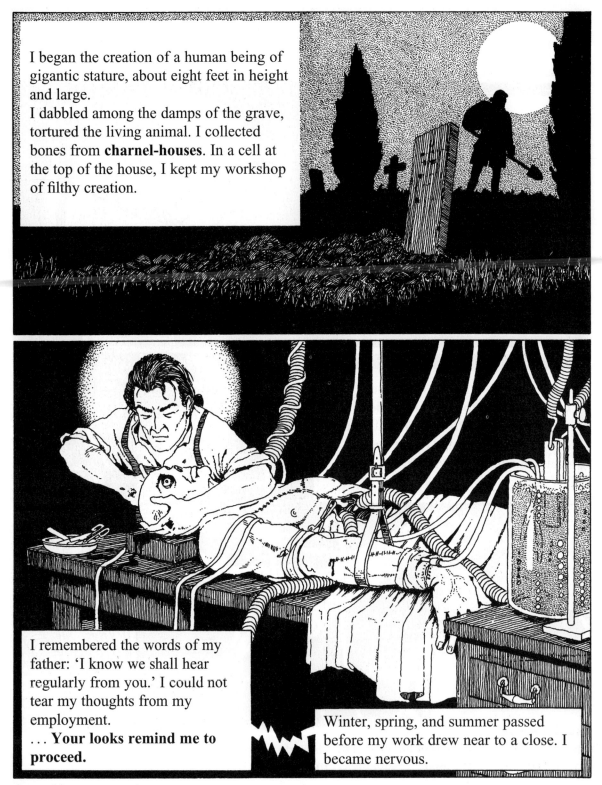

I began the creation of a human being of gigantic stature, about eight feet in height and large.
I dabbled among the damps of the grave, tortured the living animal. I collected bones from **charnel-houses**. In a cell at the top of the house, I kept my workshop of filthy creation.

I remembered the words of my father: 'I know we shall hear regularly from you.' I could not tear my thoughts from my employment.
... **Your looks remind me to proceed.**

Winter, spring, and summer passed before my work drew near to a close. I became nervous.

charnel-houses – tombs
Your looks remind me to proceed – Walton gives Frankenstein a look to remind him to continue with his tale.

Frankenstein makes his human being, but it turns out to be a monster!

It was on a night of November. I collected the instruments of life around me. The lifeless thing lay at my feet. It was one in the morning; the rain pattered against the panes, my candle was nearly burnt out. I saw the dull yellow eye of the creature open.

His yellow skin, his hair black and flowing, his teeth a pearly whiteness, but his watery eyes and black lips! Horror and disgust filled my heart.

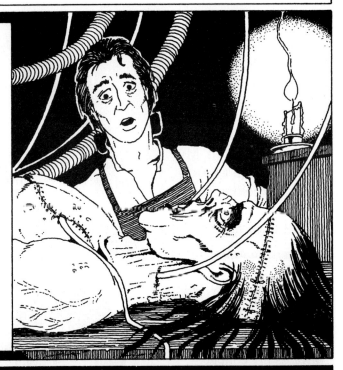

I rushed out of the room and threw myself on the bed. I slept but I was disturbed by the wildest dreams. I started from my sleep with horror – the monster held up the curtain of the bed, his eyes were fixed upon me. His jaws were opened, he muttered, a grin wrinkled his cheeks. One hand was stretched out. I escaped and rushed down stairs.

Frankenstein runs away from the monster. He meets his friend Clerval and takes him to his home. He becomes ill and Clerval nurses him until he is better.

I dare not return to the apartment. I continued walking not daring to look about me. I came at length opposite to the inn at which carriages stopped. My eyes fixed on a coach that was coming towards me. Henry Clerval sprung out.

My dear Frankenstein, how glad I am to see you.

I grasped his hand and in a moment forgot my horror. I welcomed my friend and we walked towards my college.

Tell me how you left my father, brothers, and Elizabeth.

Very well, but how very ill you appear, so thin and pale.

I have been **engaged in one occupation**, but I hope I am free.

engaged in one occupation – busy with one thing

We soon arrived at my college. The thought made me shiver that the creature I had left in my apartment might still be there, alive and walking about. I feared that Henry should see him. I darted up, I paused. Nothing appeared. The apartment was empty. We **ascended** into my room. I jumped over the chairs, clapped my hands, laughed out loud.

ascended – climbed up   confined me – kept me inside, in bed

Elizabeth has written a letter to Frankenstein full of cheerful gossip. This helps Frankenstein feel better, and he goes off on a walking tour and returns happy.

My dear Cousin,

Clerval writes that you are getting better. I hope that you will confirm this in your own handwriting.

Ernest is in the open air, climbing hills or rowing on the lake. He should be a farmer.

Do you remember Justine Moritz? Justine was a great favourite of yours. She was called home by her mother, who died at the beginning of last winter. Justine has returned to us. She is very clever and gentle.

William is very tall of his age. I have written myself into good spirits. Victor, write yourself and make all of us happy.

Elizabeth

Dear Elizabeth!
I will write instantly.

In another fortnight I was able to lave my chamber. Henry had changed my apartment. I had a dislike for my laboratory. Sciences! I disliked the subject! I hated my former studies.

Summer passed. Winter was spent cheerfully.

The month of May had already commenced. Henry proposed a tour of Ingolstadt. We passed a fortnight: my health restored.

Clerval taught me to love nature and the cheerful faces of children.

We returned to our college on a Sunday afternoon. I bounded along with feelings of joy.

Another letter arrives, and Frankenstein learns his brother William has been murdered. He goes home and thinks that he sees the monster. He is sure the monster is the murderer.

My dear Victor,

I wish to prepare you for **woeful** news. William is murdered.

Last Thursday, my niece and your two brothers went to walk. William and Ernest had gone on before. Ernest came and said that William had run away to hide, but he did not return. Elizabeth **conjectured** he might have returned to the house. He was not there. We returned again with torches. About five in the morning, I discovered my lovely boy stretched on the grass, the print of the murderer's fingers was on his neck. Elizabeth told me that William had teased her to let him wear a very valuable **miniature** of your mother. The picture is gone.

Come, Victor, you alone can **console** Elizabeth.

Alphonse Frankenstein

What do you intend to do?

Go to Geneva.

woeful – sad   **conjectured** – guessed   **miniature** – small picture   **console** – comfort

14

As I drew nearer home I resolved to visit the spot where my poor William had been murdered.

I perceived a figure. I could not be mistaken – its shape, its gigantic stature, the filthy demon to whom I had given life. HE was the murderer!

It was about five in the morning when I entered my father's house. I went into the library. Ernest entered.

How is my poor Elizabeth?

She accused herself of having caused the death of my brother. The murderer has been discovered.

No one would believe it at first. Justine Moritz so extremely wicked?

Justine Moritz! No one believes it, surely?

The morning on which the murder of poor William had been discovered, Justine had been taken ill. One of the servants discovered in her pocket the picture of my mother. Justine was charged.

I know the murderer. Poor Justine is innocent

Papa, Victor says he knows who was the murderer or poor William.

We do also.

You are mistaken. Justine is innocent.

We were soon joined by Elizabeth.

She is innocent, my Elizabeth.

I knew it.

If she is innocent, rely on the judges.

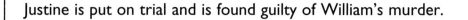

Justine is put on trial and is found guilty of William's murder.

Eleven o'clock the trial was to commence. The appearance of Justine was calm.

The trial began. Justine was called on for her defence.

She had passed the evening of the night on which the murder had been committed at the house of an aunt. At about nine o'clock she met a man who asked her if she had seen anything of a child who was lost. She passed several hours looking for him. When the gates of Geneva were shut, she was forced to remain several hours of the night in a barn.

Concerning the picture she could give no account.

Several witnesses were called. They spoke well of her. Elizabeth desired permission to address the court.

I know her. I have lived in the same house with her. She nursed my aunt in her last illness and her own mother. She was beloved by all the family. She was to the child who is now dead like a mother. I believe and rely on her innocence.

I believed in her innocence; I knew it. The demon had murdered my brother. I rushed out of the court in agony.

In the morning I went to the court.

The ballots had been thrown; they were all black and Justine was condemned.

endured – felt

Words cannot convey an idea of the heart-sickening despair that I then **endured**.

Frankenstein and Elizabeth visit Justine in prison. She must die. Frankenstein feels terrible about this.

My cousin, she has confessed.

The poor victim expressed a wish to see Elizabeth. We entered the gloomy prison.

Do you believe that I am so wicked?

But your own confession?

I confessed a lie. My confessor threatened until I almost began to think that I was the monster that he said I was.

Oh Justine! Forgive me. Yet you must die!

After Justine's death, the family go to Belrive, then to Chamounix where they hope to feel happier.

We retired to our house at Belrive. Often I took the boat and passed many hours upon the lake. I wept. I lived in fear! The monster!

I wished to see him again and avenge the deaths of William and Justine. My father's health was shaken. Elizabeth was no longer happy. My father proposed that we should all make **an excursion** to the valley of Chamounix.

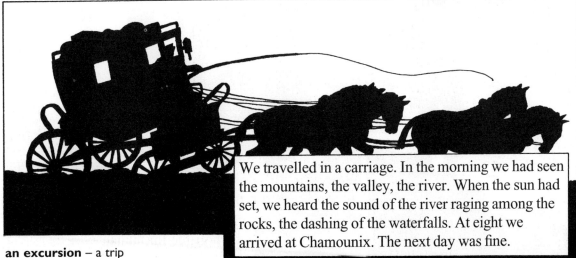

We travelled in a carriage. In the morning we had seen the mountains, the valley, the river. When the sun had set, we heard the sound of the river raging among the rocks, the dashing of the waterfalls. At eight we arrived at Chamounix. The next day was fine.

an excursion – a trip

The following morning the rain poured. I resolved to go alone to the summit of Montanvert. It was nearly noon when I arrived at the top. I sat upon the rock that overlooks the sea of ice.

I suddenly beheld the figure of a man advancing towards me with superhuman speed. I was troubled.

It was the wretch whom I had created. He approached. Its ugliness too horrible for human eyes.

purpose – plan **virtuous** – good and kind **scourge** – someone who punishes

23

The monster explains how he felt and what happened to him after Frankenstein ran away.

We crossed the ice. We entered the hut.

Seating myself by the fire, he began his tale.

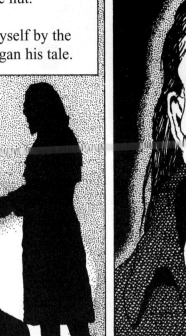

I saw, felt, heard and smelt. I could wander. I felt hunger and thirst. I was miserable. I sat down and wept. I longed to obtain food and shelter. I perceived a hut. I entered. An old man sat in it preparing his breakfast. He turned and shrieked loudly and ran across the fields. I arrived at a village, but children shrieked and one of the women fainted. The whole village was **roused**; some fled, some attacked me.

Bruised by stones I escaped to a low **hovel**. This hovel joined a cottage.

In one corner sat an old man. The young girl was arranging the cottage. The young man returned.

I longed to join them, but dared not. I would remain quietly in my hovel.

roused – woken up   **hovel** – dirty old building

24

The monster watches the people who live in the cottage, and tries to learn their language. He does jobs for then, but they don't know it's him. They have never seen him.

The cottagers were not entirely happy. I discovered one of the causes was poverty. During the night I often took tools and brought home **firing**. The first time I did this, the young woman when she opened the door in the morning appeared greatly astonished.

I perceived that the words they spoke produced pleasure or pain. I discovered the names given to some objects. I learned fire, milk, bread and wood, sister or Agatha, father, Felix, brother or son.

Felix read to the old man and Agatha. I did not even understand **the sounds for which they stood as signs**.

firing – firewood   **the sounds . . . signs** – the words from the writing on the page

I longed to **discover** myself to the cottagers.

But I was terrified when I viewed myself in a pool! At first I started back. I was the monster.

My life was spent observing my friends. I collected fuel for the cottage. I cleared their paths of snow. I heard the words good spirit, wonderful. I imagined I should **win their favour**, and afterwards their love.

discover – show   **win their favour** – get them to like me

26

A lady friend arrives at the cottage. She can't speak their language, but as she is taught it, the monster listens from its hiding place and learns it too.

The weather became fine. On one of these days, when my cottagers rested from labour, someone tapped at the door. It was a lady on horseback. She held out her hand to Felix who kissed it and called her his sweet Arabian.

The stranger appeared to have a language of her own. I found she was **endeavouring** to learn their language. The idea occurred to me that I should make use of the same instructions.

I improved in speech. I learned of father, mother, brother, sister. Where were my friends and relations? What was I? Who was I? Questions I was unable to solve.

I discovered some papers in the pocket of the **dress** which I had taken from your laboratory. I began to study them.

Why did you form a monster so hideous that even you turned from me in disgust?

What a wretched outcast I was.

endeavouring – trying   **dress** – clothes

27

The monster plans to introduce himself to the cottagers. The old man is blind, so at first things go well. The plan goes badly wrong when the others return.

One day the old man was left alone. I approached the door of their cottage.

Who is there?

I am a traveller.

Enter.

I am going to claim the protection of some friends. These people know little of me. I am full of fears for if I fail there I am an outcast in the world forever.

If these friends are good, do not despair. May I know the names of these friends?

I sank on the chair and sobbed aloud.

The monster gets angry, but he decides to try again. He finds the family has left. He burns the cottage and sets off to find Frankenstein.

Why did I live? My feelings were those of rage and revenge – more than all, against him who had formed me.

I resolved to return to the cottage. The inside was dark. I heard no motion.

Felix approached with another man.

The life of my father is in the greatest danger. My wife and sister will never recover their horror. Let me fly from this place.

I never saw them more. Anger returned.

I quitted the scene. The thought of you crossed my mind and towards this place I resolved to proceed.

He travels but finds that people are scared of him. He explains how he murdered William and planted evidence on Justine.

I travelled only at night and found no shelter. Snow fell and the waters hardened but I rested not.

The earth again began to look green. I continued among the paths of the wood. I heard the sound of voices.

A young girl came running ...

... her foot slipped and she fell into the stream.

I rushed from my hiding place and saved her.

A **rustic** aimed a gun and fired.

The miserable pain of wound gave way to hellish rage. I vowed hatred to all mankind.

rustic – farmworker

After some weeks my wound healed and I continued my journey. I reached the **environs** of Geneva.

A sleep was disturbed by a beautiful child who came running. If I could seize him as my friend I should not be so **desolate**.

I do not intend to hurt you; listen to me.

Let me go! Monster! You wish to eat me, and tear me to pieces. Let me go or I will tell my papa.

Boy, you will never see your father again; you must come with me.

Let me go. My papa is M. Frankenstein – he would punish you. You dare not keep me.

Frankenstein! You belong to my enemy. You shall be my first victim.

The child struggled. I grasped his throat to silence him and in a moment he lay dead at my feet.

environs – outskirts   **desolate** – miserable

32

Frankenstein agrees to marry Elizabeth, but he wants to visit England with his friend, Clerval. He plans to make the female monster during the two years he is away.

Week after week passed. I spent whole days on the lake.

It was after one of these rambles that my father addressed me.

I have always looked forward to your marriage with your cousin. You perhaps regard her as your sister without any wish that she might become your wife. Tell me whether you object to marriage.

I must **perform my engagement** and let the monster depart with his mate before I allow myself to **enjoy a union**.

I expressed a wish to visit England before I **sat** down for life. Our plan was soon arranged. Clerval would join me and the tour should occupy two years. Elizabeth approved.

perform my engagement – create the female monster   **enjoy a union** – get married   **sat** – settled

Clerval and Frankenstein travel across Europe to Scotland. Frankenstein goes alone to the Orkneys to carry on with his secret project.

I remembered to order that my chemical instruments should be packed to go with me. I resolved to fulfil my promise and return a free man.

We travelled ... Switzerland, Holland, England ... at length we saw London.

I began to collect the materials for my new creation.

After some months in London, we received a letter from a person in Scotland. We quitted London.

A few days at Windsor, to Oxford, to Matlock, Cumberland and Westmoreland, Edinburgh and Perth where our friend expected us.

I told Clerval I wished to make the tour of Scotland alone.

I fixed on the Orkneys. On the whole of the island there were three miserable huts and one of these was vacant. This I hired.

I proceeded in my labour. It became more horrible. Sometimes I could not enter my laboratory for days.

I grew nervous. I worked on.

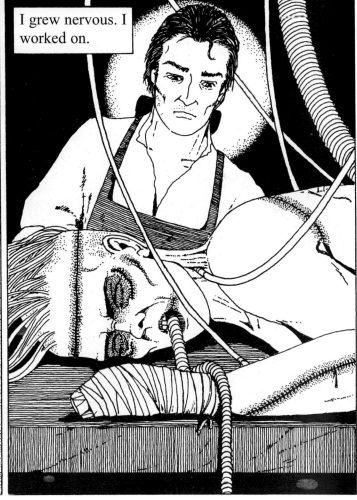

Frankenstein has second thoughts about the female monster. He destroys what he has done and the monster threatens him.

I was now about to form another being ... HE had sworn to quit the neighbourhood of man, but she had not!

They might hate each other. She might turn with disgust from him. The wickedness of my promise burst upon me.

I trembled. Looking up I saw the demon at the **casement**. He had followed me.

casement – window

The wretch saw me destroy the creature. He, with a howl of revenge, withdrew.

My ear was arrested by – I heard   **I am firm** – I've made up my mind

Frankenstein leaves the Orkneys but gets swept away to Ireland where is arrested for murder.

Before I departed I must pack my chemical instruments. The remains of the half-finished creature lay scattered on the floor. I put them into a basket with stones.

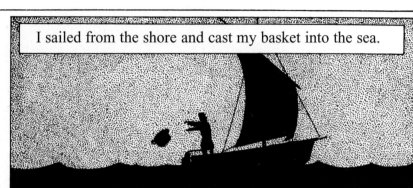

I sailed from the shore and cast my basket into the sea.

I stretched myself at the bottom of the boat and in a short time I slept.

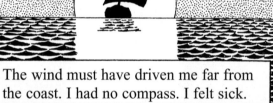

The wind must have driven me far from the coast. I had no compass. I felt sick.

Suddenly I saw a line of high land. I steered my course towards the land. I perceived a good harbour which I entered.

People crowded, whispered together.

Will you be so kind as to tell me the name of this town?

You will know that soon enough, but **you will not be consulted as to your quarters**. The Irish hate villains.

Follow me to Mr Kirwin's.

Who is Mr Kirwin?

Mr Kirwin is a magistrate. You are to give an account of the death of a gentleman who was found murdered here last night.

I was innocent, that could be easily proved. I followed in silence.

you will not ... your quarters. – you won't be asked where you want to stay.

Henry Clerval has been murdered! Frankenstein blames himself. He is thrown into prison, but the magistrate is kind and sends for Frankenstein's father.

The magistrate asked who appeared as witnesses.

One **deposed** he had been out fishing. They did not land at the harbour but at a creek. He walked along the sands. He struck his foot against something.

They found the body of a man. The clothes were not wet. He had been strangled.

There was no sign of violence except black marks of fingers on his neck.

I remembered the murder of my brother.

A woman saw a boat with only one man in it.

Mr Kirwin desired that I should be taken into the room where the body lay. I was led up to the coffin. I saw Henry Clerval stretched out before me. I gasped.

deposed – stated

Two I have already destroyed. Other victims wait! Clerval my friend.

sessions – trials at the court   dress – clothes

Frankenstein is set free. He and his father travel to Paris where he receives a letter from Elizabeth. He writes a letter back. The wedding will go ahead and a secret will be told!

The case was not brought before the court, on its being proved that I was on the Orkney Islands at the hour the body of my friend was found. I was liberated from prison.

He may be innocent of the murder, but he has a bad conscience.

Yes I had one: William, Justine and Clerval had died. Whose death is to finish the tragedy?

union – marriage

Paris ... I received the following letter from Elizabeth

My dear Friend,

How much you must have suffered! You well know that our **union** had been the favourite plan of your parents. We were told this when young, and taught to look forward to it.

Answer me. Do you not love another? I love you, but it is your happiness I desire as well as my own. My uncle will send me news of your health, and if I see but one smile on your lips when we meet, I shall need no other happiness.

Elizabeth

44

I wrote to Elizabeth.

To you alone do I **consecrate** my life. I have one secret. It will chill your frame with horror. I will confide this tale of misery and terror to you the day after our marriage shall take place.
Until then do not mention it.

We returned to Geneva. My cousin welcomed me.

When I thought on what had passed, sometimes I was furious; sometimes low and **despondent**. Elizabeth alone had the power to soothe me.

consecrate – dedicate   **despondent** – depressed

On the night of the marriage the monster murders again. His threat is carried out!

My father spoke of the immediate marriage. To me the remembrance of the threat returned.

I shall be with you on your wedding night.

Preparations were made. I carried pistols and a dagger.

After the ceremony a large party assembled at my father's. It was agreed that Elizabeth and I should pass the afternoon and night at Evian and we resolved to go by water. We landed and as I touched the shore I felt those fears. We walked for a short time then retired to the inn.

Victor? What is it you fear?

This night is dreadful.

I entreated her to retire. She left me and I continued some time walking up and down the house inspecting every corner.

Suddenly I heard a scream.

It came from the room into which Elizabeth had retired.

The scream was repeated and I rushed into the room.

I entreated her to retire. – I asked her to go to bed.

Frankenstein tells a judge about the monster and then decides to track him. He goes to the graveyard before he sets off.

My father could not live under the horrors and in a few days he died.

I **repaired to** a judge in town and told him I knew the destroyer of my family. I related my history.

I would willingly **afford you every aid**, but who can follow an animal which can **traverse** the sea of ice, and inhabit caves and dens where no man would venture?

You do not **credit my narrative**.

You are mistaken. If it is in my power to seize the monster he shall suffer punishment.

I devote myself to his destruction

repaired to – went to   **afford you every aid** – give you my help   **traverse** – cross
credit my narrative – believe my story

reposed – were buried

Frankenstein follows the monster until he finds Walton's ship.

I pursued him. The Mediterranean, the Black Sea, Russia. I have followed his track. Sometimes he left markings in writing on the barks of trees or cut in stone.

The snows thickened. The rivers were covered with ice.

I **procured** a sledge and dogs.

I arrived at a **hamlet**. A gigantic monster had arrived the night before armed with a gun and pistols. It had carried off their store of winter food and had seized a drove of dogs and had pursued his journey across the sea that led to no land. I departed.

procured – bought   **hamlet** – small village

Walton has problems with the ice trapping his ship. When it melts, he decides to go home. Frankenstein dies.

A week passed while I have listened.

September 2nd

My beloved Sister,

I am surrounded by mountains of ice which threaten to crush my vessel. We may not survive.

September 5th

This morning sailors entered and their leader addressed me. They desired I should promise that if the vessel should be freed, I would direct my course southward.

September 12th

It is past; I am returning to England. I have lost my hopes of glory. I have lost my friend. The ice began to move.

renew that request – ask again

I am interrupted. There is a sound. It comes from the cabin where the remains of Frankenstein still lie.

I enter the cabin. Over him hung a form gigantic in stature, his face was concealed by long locks of ragged hair. He sprung towards the window.

I called on him to stay.

Farewell Frankenstein! Farewell!

He sprung from the cabin window upon the ice raft which lay close to the vessel. He was soon borne away by the waves and lost in darkness and distance.

THE END